The Ice Fair

by Ryan Fadus   illustrated by Scott A. Scheidly

Orlando   Boston   Dallas   Chicago   San Diego

Visit *The Learning Site!*

www.harcourtschool.com

Printed in China

ISBN 0-15-325491-2

15 16 17 18 19 20 985 10 09 08 07 06

Ordering Options
ISBN 0-15-325468-8 (Collection)
ISBN 0-15-326569-8 (package of 5)

 I want to ride on the ice slide.
Where can I buy a ticket?

 Hand me one ice cube.
Now you can go.
Take a ride on the slide.

Can I buy a ticket? I want to walk in the ice maze.

4

 Hand me one ice cube.
Now you can go.
Have fun in the maze!

 I want to win a big prize.
Can I play the game?

6

 Hand me one ice cube.
Now you can play the game.

 You win the big prize!